Embracing The Fall

Margo LaGattuta
Art by Christine Reising

11/11/01

Plain View Press
P.O. Box 33311
Austin, TX 78764
512-441-2452

*For Michéle,
Embracing your
creativity!
Best,
Margo
LaGattuta*

Many thanks to the Ragdale Foundation for the writing time, for the fall and the embrace...

Other books by Margo LaGattuta: *Diversion Road* (1983, State Street Press, Brockport, New York), *Noedgelines* (1986, Earhart Press, Ann Arbor, Michigan), and *The Dream Givers* (1990, Lake Shore Publishing, Deerfield, Illinois).

Cover art: "Keeper of the Secret," mixed media sculpture, 1993, Christine Reising.
Graphic Artist for cover: Jeanne Kero

ACKNOWLEDGMENTS

My thanks for creative support and insightful criticism to Susan Bright, Alice Friman, Betty Grahn, Lee Grue, Mary Hebert, Faye Kicknosway, Judith Kitchen, Kay Lister, Gail Mally-Mack, Angelica Melfi, Christine Reising, Lois Robbins, Gay Rubin, Bill Shippey, Carol Spelius, Ann Williamson, and The First Thursday Group.

Poems in this book originally appeared in *Yankee*, *MidAmerica XVII*, *The Bridge*, *5AM*, *Mobius*, *Ecologic*, *Ohio Poetry Day Awards Anthology*, *PhenomeNews*, and the *National Federation of State Poetry Societies Awards Anthology*.

Award-winning poems include: "Embracing the Fall" (1991 Gwendolyn Brooks Award, Michigan State University), "I Vacuum, Therefore I Am (1993 Sisters of the Heart Award, First Prize, National Federation of State Poetry Societies), "Surfacing" (1993 Power of Woman Award, First Prize, National Federation of State Poetry Societies), "Scene Talking" (1992 Florida State Poet's Association Award, Second Prize, NFSPS), "Roll the Reel Backwards" (1992 Founder's Award, Honorable Mention, NFSPS), "Used Clothes" (1990 Herman & Miriam Lepp Memorial Award, First Prize, Ohio Poetry Day Awards), "Memo" (1990 In memory of Heidi Knecht Award, First Prize, Ohio Poetry Day Awards), "Prayers for the Dead and the Living" (1993 New Beginnings Award, Ohio Poetry Day Awards), "Beat the Deadline - or Lose Out!" and "The Usual and the Unsung" (1993 Ohio Poetry Day Awards).

These poems appeared and traveled with the "Noedgelines" art exhibit, a collaboration with visual artist Christine Reising: "Grace," "Heart Spills," " You Can Get to Total from Here," "Getting Lost," and "The Bird Inside."

This book is dedicated to my three suns: Mark, Erik and Adam.

Contents

III. HEART SPILLS 59

FOREWORD

I once read in the **Chicago Tribune** that the cure for fainting is falling, that we must fall down in order to rise up again clear-headed. That wonderful paradox, and how we embrace it, led to many poems in this book.

I.

OWNING THE FIRE

Real or imagined, the heat had to be ours.
To own it was a kind of terrible dance.

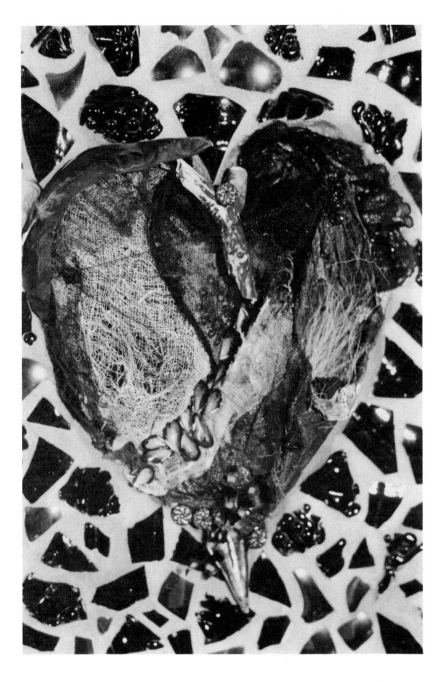

"Grieving the Illusion, 3" (detail) mixed media, wall piece
Christine Reising, 1992

OWNING THE FIRE

The night we heard there was a fire,
and we saw no fire, some of us laughed.
But we all cleared out. Poets were just
stopped in mid breath. Stanzas hung
in the air like smoke. "In this dream,"

we wondered, "is the burning roof real,
or are we all part of a group metaphor?
Has the power of our hot illusions
finally brought us to this?"
We entered the night like homeless pigeons

clutching whatever we thought to save,
clutching a clock, a book, a raincoat.
How the mind races blindly toward loss.
Some of us couldn't think fast enough
to name what we could live without.

Some of us flipped through old losses
like a spiral phone book of recalled friends.
We wondered where to place this new fire.
Real or imagined, the heat had to be ours.
To own it was a kind of terrible dance.

ROLL THE REEL BACKWARDS

and it's a home movie in Key
Biscayne, Florida. I'm sixteen
and my ripening body dives
into a Ramada Inn pool.
I am fruit and the young man at 7-11
picks me. See me waiting for hours
at the phone booth. See him
never show up for our date.

Roll the reel backwards
and he never calls, never catches
his eye on my black bathing suit.
Water leaps into the air; the pool
spits me, feet first, up
onto the diving board, and I am
dry and moving slowly back,
back before his mouth against my mouth,
before a word allows itself loose.

Roll the reel backwards;
let the word soak up its own
connotations, its own cough;
go all the way back, before thought
or even a frame of picture.
See the word eat its own desire.

Word begins its long
sad journey back, before desire
ripens on the tongue. See the
picture spliced, a jump
cut of light memory erased. See un-
sweetened memory dissolve in its own juice.

Roll the reel backwards;
see the start — a gray flicker, a flower,
a blurred hum of light, and dust's
random dance against a
6 . . . 5 . . . 4 . . .3 . . .
click click click click click

THE EAGLE SPREAD

I used to hang from the tops
of monkey bars when I was a
Detroit kid. My best friend
Lynne taught me the Eagle Spread.
Hung upside down by hands and knees,
you arched your back slowly
till your stretched body looked
like a capital letter U.

Facing the earth, it was like
flying over the slanted world
of Hartwell Street, an aerial act
impressing little Richie Ferguson,
who came to our three ring circus
but wouldn't play caged gorilla.
I watched Sue be a lion. She
jumped head first through a pink
Hula Hoop, dazzling me with daring.

Everything looked smaller as I
flew over my Howdy Doody life.
I saw myself roller skating between
cracks in the sidewalk, knowing
I'd break my mother's back –
if I overstepped just one.

Dolls prettier than we were
let us cut and curl their hair.
We dressed them up in scarves,
taught them how to be wives.
Barbie gave birth in the sandbox,
after a long, invented labor.

I played spin-the-time-bottle,
kissing freckle-faced Bobby
till I felt like it mattered,
till he learned I wasn't Jewish,

and Mom found naked drawings
buried under our family bushes.

Now he's an eye surgeon
with a wife and three kids.
Lynne lives in Waterford,
teaching low impact aerobics,
and I'm still up here hanging
from my childhood circus,
trying to fly like an eagle
over the tops of all those times.

THE MAN FROM THE ATTIC

Looking back I see him
lurking in the shadows of my
first kiss, the man who fed me
silver spoonfuls of my own dread.

He was a ragged watcher,
beggar and fiend, who wanted
me more than even a Harley.
In the attic rafters

I'd flash my brazen body,
let him steal a look
from behind the innocent wall
of starlight between us.

I loved his invisible eyes
that pierced the night window.
I loved my own floating
fear of him, like making myself read

the S Volume of the *Book of Knowledge*
and touching all the pictures of snakes.
Meanwhile the sounds of "Dragnet" and
"I Remember Mama" drifted up the stairs.

He courted me through all
my early romances, through
Bobby Blau and the giddy
basement kissing parties, through

tossing Bob Matthews his high school
ring in the frozen food section at Krogers,
He even sang "Stardust" off-key
under the queen-sized discomfort
of my shattering first marriage.

Nothing can stop him.
Into the stretch-marks of my
middle years, he is now leering.
He is closer than a contact lens,

watching me, sending me dark roses,
dancing me fiercely into his heart.

PEOPLE HUGGING

A sand path along the Gulf shore
reveals a broken piece of coral,
and I am transported to an
earlier scene. An old woman
with large hands is serving
Swedish meatballs. Her voice comes
into my ear in smooth
brown waves. Arms around

arms, people hugging is the
memory then. A man whistles
for a dog, who romps along
sniffing some berry bushes,
to a path that curls inward.

I look at my bent feet
in sand walking on sharp
stones and cut shells.
This coral in my hand
looks like a foot walking
slowly up a wall, and I am
walking up the wall of my

childhood. My grandmother's
hands tuck a shawl around my
shoulders. An old Victrola
playing waltzes on the porch
returns my ear to the farmhouse
sounds of wild kittens in the
cellar. Grandmother plays
another 78. This time it's
"Hallelujah, I'm a Bum,"
and Pete Grease, one of the
hoboes from Hawthorne Street,
presses a dirty penny in my
arched hand. He hugs me tightly,
stands in her diaphanous kitchen

slurping Sanka with cream and honey,
spreading toast with raspberry jam.

A sea gull squawks and lands
on a stump. Two people hugging
on the beach startle, as I
pass. Murky broken shells
hug the sand and are suddenly,
like an instant breath of memory,
washed clean by the next wave.

TRUSTING THE LAKE

She floats, her eyes above water, in a black inner tube.
It will hold me up, she thinks. A ten-year-old girl,
floating in Lake Manchog is hugging the air.
Waves roll by; she has no idea what's ahead,

but she likes the lightness of clear water.
Even the rain tickles her round face.
She has already caught a glimpse into time,
not all the particulars, but the pattern of things
to come. There is a joy ahead, she can hardly

wait for it, but the sorrows are dark pollywogs
hiding like the marshy roots in a nearby bog.
If she knew them all, she'd spring a leak,
jump overboard and sink into the lost palace,

but the camera has a way of keeping her innocent,
expectancy and joy in her near-sighted eyes.
Her hair, parted in the middle, is drawn
back into braids, woven together like the two
sides of herself, grief and ecstasy a blend
of inner parts wound round and round, then
bound with a silver elastic knot at the end.

We leave her there floating, in an old photo
album. She is suspended forever in that young
moment, that hopeful buoyant pose on the lake.
It will take her years to get it back,
that way of trusting the waves to hold her,
of trusting her own delicate inner luck.

WASHING THE TOMBSTONE

Beyond the plastic geraniums,
ferns and planted impatiens,
Mother and I find the mossy headstone.
He was a designer, she remembers,
sadly viewing the weathered monument.
He would be glad we've planted real flowers.

Today, we stand in Fairview Cemetery
with a bucket of suds. *Here,*
she says, *You do one side,*
and I'll do the other,
handing me the scrub brush;
and I count almost seven
years from the date we had
carved into smooth marble.

Brushing aside fallen bark,
weeds, a few loose branches,
I begin to wash bird droppings
from the grooves of my father's
good name. A twig is stuck
in the letter E of Edwin. Mother
scrapes it with a fingernail.
I scour his epitaph: "A Man
with Enough Love for Everyone,"
feel the rough and smooth edges.

Now we both dip our hands
into fresh warm water
and rinse the memories clean.

SMALL BOATS IN MY ROOM

In complete stillness, a stone girl is dancing.
Zen Master Seung Sahn

The love I hold back
sits in an overstuffed arm-
chair reading Lao-Tzu and
sipping French Roast. On the wall

a shoreline hangs suspended.
Three tiny women in white
babushkas stand waiting
for small boats to arrive
or dissolve into the horizon.

Everything stops ticking at
once in this scene, even
the dancing words pull back
(clear water has no taste)

and enter the stillness of sailboats
on the wall, neither coming
home yet or leaving. Picture
me in this stone room waving.

SIX WAYS TO LOOK AT A PEAR

from Wallace Stevens

1. One ripe pear, alone on a table, is jazz playing
   in the apartment downstairs. A soft sound,
   like an old pear, is sweeter than mellow juice.

2. Two Bosc pears are a man and a woman talking,
   an argument. A rough brown word passes
   between them in the night air.

3. The bumps of pears, like cellulite on thighs,
   are tired women doing aerobics in a damp room.

4. Pears are bruised roads in Ohio, leading
   around in circles. Pears are pulling us home.

5. The torn skin of a green pear reveals its
   story. The stem grows out of the memory of trees.
   The pear takes loss in its stride.

6. Looking at pears is the anticipation of feeling.
   Pears get down to basics. Green thoughts are the
   hope of new pears in a basket. The power of things
   swallowed. The satisfaction of future bees.

THE USUAL AND THE UNSUNG

The magician juggles apples; she
knows that to keep them in the air
she must stay amazed and never
think of falling. Her apples

must be rosy and always fly
up at a rate, like the usual
buoyancy of wind, faster than hard
cores of doubt could be

falling. She must keep her
eye always on the grouping,
her ear on that whir of apple,
and ignore any rumbling a hard

floor makes as it pulls
against a rush of flying
apple threads. A floor calling
apples is seductive, but a shining

apple in the air is a moving
window, a space through which
any gentle juggler might see
delicacy and grace in the unsung
heart of an ordinary apple.

THE ASHTRAY OF LOVE

Love dies in a little fire
grown smaller in its own dish.
It is the dish inside the room
where a tired bear lives and
eats his dim heart's breakfast.

This bear sits in a stiff chair
for this, porridge waiting but
unwelcome as a cold
lumpy regret tastes foul.
Last night's smoke lingers

in the morning ashtray,
our bear barely remembering
the fire that burned itself
out in the dish rumored
to be the least likely hollow

for a heart to find love in.
And the love inside the love
that is not there in the ashtray
inside the little tomb of brittle
bear, contains the echo of faint hope,
a prism of lost fires blazing.

EATING PEARS

Down to the core, around
in circles, eating pears
is a delicate act of surrender.
Some teeth won't march through
thin layers of matte-finished skin.

Not glossy like apples,
pears want to keep out cowards
who shun a rough textured
Bosc fuzz on their tongues.

Only the willing riskers
need enter private pears,
hoping for a torn sweetness.

THE ONE WHO SAID NO

I knew you wanted some.
That wet burrito was too big
for me to eat all alone.
Smothered in jack cheese,

black olives and jalapenas,
it overflowed the plate
and offered itself to you.
But, no, you said,

content with your usual BLT.
Not hungry, you watched
from your distant chair
as I slathered on sour cream.

I was eating it slow and colorful.
I was eating only from my own dish,
pretending I didn't notice you,
stone still, the hint of drool forming
on your stubborn lip.

ECLIPSE

You and I stood like that
with all our clothes on
watching the moon, the moon
more naked than we. We

stood with all the others
that night on the prairie,
shadow of the earth creeping
across its own fat moon.

We talked of moon things,
but no one knew what
it meant, this cover-up,
this moving pillow case,

or how long it would take
for a whole fat moon to be
eaten alive in the night,
one full shining meal.

We stood, the shadows
of our very selves covering
each of us, and waited
for the effacement to end.

CONSUMED

Somewhere in the Milky Way
at the very center of a black hole
is a galactic Chinese dragon
more powerful than ten million suns.

They say he's gobbling up stars
in a blast of energy like a hot
breath. One star every five thousand
years gets swallowed in dust.

Call him Sagittarius A.
They say he sits on a relentless
throne eating bunches of hot
giant stars. He has no mercy.

You'd think the stars would
figure it out, after awhile
quit twinkling at the old boy,
grab a plane to Kansas City.

I guess the stars were made to glitter.
They just can't stop edging closer
to the seductive pull.
The afterglow must be worth it.

HIDDEN ADMIRER

One who admires you greatly is hidden before your eyes.
Fortune Cookie

Disguised as a chair
the hidden admirer stands
objectively in your boudoir.
He is frank and alone,
wooden in his attempts to court you.

His fluttering can't be seen
easily with the naked eye,
a natural veneer covering his
heart murmurs, his worn interior.

Even the Venetian blind
covering the darkest bay window
can't see what love's venal
bargain has done to this chair.

He waits for you to walk by.
The touch of your velour robe
comforts him, sets him to
dreaming in place, silently
worries the air around his face.

The chair thinks, if only he
could hold you without your
knowing what he feels, if
only he could feel without
holding you at all. This

secret makes the cats nervous.
They leap and spin across
the room, fly at the chair's
still life, making mayhem
of such interior design.

THE BRIDE IS EMBRACED BY A GOAT

*from Marc Chagall's painting,
"Midsummer Night's Dream"*

Her white skin wrinkled
a little, she keeps a straight
face and holds her fan just so.

The bride is stunned by her own
stillness. A calm white as a lace
gown enters her body through the heart.

A man flies over her head in a red
outfit with wings flapping, knocks on her
hairdo screaming about the future.

In a nearby tree, a bright
bird sits oblivious to the whole
picture, while behind the goat's

pungent smile lurks a green
person slicing and eating sour
apples that taste like the past.

STRING AFFAIR

One string is waiting
to be looped by another.
It is trying the impossible trick
of hanging free around a box
of Chinese wind socks,
pretending not to want
closure, or anything that
seductive. Just a frayed
end flapping in the breeze.
Just a white moment
pausing to reflect upon
its own significant other
string, which is nowhere
to be found in this
package. Not to be
undone or tied up
is the string's peace now.
Not to be seen wanting
gives a certain twist on grief.

A CHINESE TABLE

A man and a woman stand on a hill.
They are embedded in a wooden·
table top, worn smooth by years
of tea cups. A cup of Earl
Grey tea is placed over
their heads, their stationary bodies.

The man has no face.
In his right hand he
holds a lantern, or is it
a vase of gardenias? But
he cannot see them at all.
He is deep in his own silence.

The woman, her arms folded,
is calm. With one eye she
watches the man. The other
eye is closed, her face in
repose, as if an alert sleep
has taken her momentarily away.
There are fish in her apron.

They have lived for years in
this flat Chinese table, their
bodies worn smooth by
the biscuits and light
conversation passing over them.
They never touch, but the
sleeves of their garments,

the deliberate silk that drapes
the air between them. It makes
a sound of gardenias passing
through cloth, the sole
connection, their only warmth.

HOW WHITE TULIPS LEAN

Planted in the same garden,
roots separate yet entwined,
they reach for the first white face.
You look like me,
they say, *and, ah*
I even love you for it.

They lean in,
and their leaning makes
the sound of silver bells happen.
Startled, they try to run.
Nowhere far enough works.

So they make a kind of game.
Lean and run. Lean and run.
Soon up to their necks
in the circle of twists and tricks,
wrapped like rope around each other's throats,

they pull the night around themselves,
a blanket of prairieblazing stars.
They call it rope burn. They call it love.

474 MEN

(a license plate)

To all the men far away
whose kisses left me with
dim sum on my lips and
the cool recollection of sheets,

may you find yourselves worthy
of long walks through my hair.
In the narrowest rooms you
let me enter, I spilled

laughter and tiny tea roses.
Mirrors flew in our faces then,
and, running helpless through
maze after maze, we all lost

our way, couldn't separate
the hearts from the trees. What
children we became in leaving.
What broken winters after the fall.

GETTING LOST

A white butterfly floats
into view as I swing
back and forth in my hammock.

You. The phone call. The letter.
Easy piano music plays Bach.
The butterfly lights on a leaf.
A bird pecks and eats. Pecks and eats.

Hiroshima feels like a place on a
hammock where I sit sipping ice.
Your voice on the phone was water.
I watch the butterfly getting lost.

Now the hammock becomes a pendulum.
Back and forth. Back and forth.
Crickets click on miniature typewriters
typing white butterflies into the air.

I remember a story of Hiroshima.
How a healing can take place after
folding one thousand paper cranes.
Pieces of my heart start folding.

I fold white paper out and in.
Back and forth. Back and forth.
I fold until I am not moving.
Cranes pile up. Release themselves.

MOVING TO MUSKEGON

Deciding to move to Muskegon took
everything I didn't have - - lamps and
shovels for digging deep rooms

in my heart. Birds of all kinds
were wheeling about in pleasure.
Muskegon was still the last place

I'd have chosen to go. Muskegon seemed
like nowhere but an empty
hole in the state I call home.

Darkness, darkness and a slow
moving river can cut
through white pines of intent.

Sometimes a place I've never
been just calls up.
The sound comes along a wire.

Sometimes where I never
thought to go whispers:
Montreal, Mozambique, or Helena, Montana,

and I have to sit stiller
than a dried up wish to hear
an electric unexpected note
like the hanging and unhanging of bells.

THROUGH THE MOVING DOORWAY

The day my home town blew up was Wednesday,
an ordinary day on anyone's Weekly Planner.
The boom was heard for fourteen miles.
There were doors and windows spinning,
folks' beds and dishes flying through air
all the way to the next town. No one
knew this could happen. All the everyday
events seemed to stop in mid-air, like the
plates and cups, the little rugs and kitchen
magnets, which were now attached to no one's
particular kitchen. *It was something to
see, all right,* said the Yogurt Shop man. *We
dove for the floor. We thought a plane crashed
through our roof. I dropped my chocolate mint
swirl and slid right under the lunch counter.*
Then the sky filled with Mr. Wilson's tax returns,
feathers, a few hats, and all the shoes you could
imagine. Shoes make a whirring sound, as they
fly through plate glass windows. *Nothing like
this ever happens on Main Street,* said the chap
who makes locks and copies keys. *Safe as any*

*suburban setting. I used to count on my town
staying put.* The Boutique on the corner blew
right through the Bicycle Store. It was on the
Six O'Clock News. All the camera crews bought
sugar doughnuts while they filmed the prisoners
sweeping up the debris. No prisoners ever lived
in my home town, except the ones who were held
captive by the walls of their minds. A few trees
got away this time, and a lamp post. Someone's
grandma was in the New Phases Beauty Shop having

her toenails done when the gas main blew up. It
shocked the curl right out of her brand new perm.
One unlucky fellow died. No one's ever died
on Main Street before. What can we count on

these days when, just as we've gotten cozy,
any one of us could be lifted up and dropped
right down in the middle of anywhere else?

In the aftermath, I drove around town
and saw a little green door on someone's
top floor. It was a living room door,
and now it opens right up to the sky.

WAITING FOR MY EYES

The angel of eyes told me
I was not seeing straight
and needed my contacts corrected.
With your right eye, please look
into the center of the circle of light.
I placed my face in his hands.
Does this red line go anywhere near
your heart?   He lit the wall.

The alphabet was climbing.
The vowels wanted to blur and mingle.
I read them like a pale song,
read them with the right eye
of a homing pigeon searching for land,
read them with my left eye for darkness,
read between the lines where
only the silences could blur.
Till, my left eye weeping,
I let my right eye tell the truth.

Worse than I thought, the angel mused.
Your naked eye is a dark boat
moving through glaciers of the wrong sea.
You don't see things.
And now I am waiting for my eyes,
waiting to clear things up, to see

what distant objects float by,
what bluer blue. What sky.

II.
WHAT EARTH KNOWS

Earth growls: *Don't stop*
me. I need to crumble
in upon myself. You'll see.
Don't try to clip my volcano.

Before it's over trees will shiver
in their very roots at my depth.
Already the worms know this,
inching their way down to the light.

"The Bird Inside," mixed media
Christine Reising, 1991

THE BIRD INSIDE

A bird, a little sparrow is enclosed.
He fell into my chimney by mistake.
The chirping started low, but now it grows.

He wonders why it's dark there, I suppose.
His song is glass that doesn't want to break.
A bird, a little sparrow is enclosed

inside the dark, but waking up he knows
that singing is the only chance to take.
The chirping started low, but now it grows

to screech and warble. Chamber music flows
with images of soaring by the lake.
A bird, a little sparrow is enclosed

with dream of sky, or so the story goes.
No song so clear could ever be a fake.
The chirping started low, but now it grows,

releasing in a breath that lifts and blows,
the purest note a bird could ever make.
A bird, a little sparrow is enclosed.
The chirping started low, but now it grows.

SACRED ROOMS

This winter day I walk
along the glass sidewalk.
No one sees me but the wind
snapping a raw willow branch in my face.

I am pushing forward.
I am pushing cold aside
to get at what is just inside
the sacred rooms in my heart.

Through this doorway, the waiting
room is red, a meadow full
of bloodroot and snakeweed. I hum
and count the hopes that fly

like wrens across the sunrise.
Another room is bare, and echoes
loss down long wooden corridors.
No song is sung by angry midgets marching.

I invite myself to leave.
I open doors and close them.
I am in the sacred place
of choosing, the winter walk
that drops me into spring.

SCENE TALKING

The iris by the house is tired,
grown too long and limped over itself.
But you, yellow oxeye daisy,
a stalk, a weed against the sky,
multiple and singular wild thing,
know that only the strongest longing
can be found in such solitude.

All the morning, light envelopes your face.
There are woods and willows.
A dark thing is drawing closer;
you cannot see its nose.

The night forces you to contract.
Everything wants you to be
firm about this silence.

Details escape you. There are
other flowers and a dozen shrill birds.
They are clean and never ending.
A stunned frog sits on the stone walk.

Each one waits for its own fullness,
to go inside the shadow and feel its dance.

OPEN LANDS

1.
Sometimes in the unexpected marsh
of a January thaw, all berries
startle and become signs.
Under ice and brittle prairie grass
a fire red branch points the way,
curled leaves soften underfoot,
and grief, my old invisible dog,
has left her prints on the path.

2.
Every prairie day new,
today a wind; old leaves
scatter and scamper like
confused squirrels. Even stiff
trees twist and wobble. Wooden
angels fly in bold
to rearrange their skirts.

3.
The day has gifts up its
trees. The slow drip
of melting thoughts. The time
it takes to open a mind
or a frozen meadow trail.
Everything moves like a
thrush moves. Sure,
impetuous and random.

IMPACT

I go to the woods to get over you.
I bite off your head
like the lady praying mantis,
chew up your whole face
while you casually sleep.

What man wouldn't
climb a tree for me?
Even the critic from Owosso
thinks I'm desirable and pithy.

I walk out of the woods, the blood
red sun hits my face. Finally, the caws of
ambivalent birds merge, a screeching chorus.
My feet swallow the softness of wet grass.

A sudden deer, caught and alert
comes in bold, then lurches left.
Larkspur and jasmine whisper and fume.

All decisions tumble and mix to the
hum of natural acts.

THE NEW IS OLD, THE OLD IS A MOON

Every dawn there dawns a dawn,
and every dawn has its eve.
Every moon there moons a moon,
and every moon is round.
Ancient Chinese Proverb

After breakfast of egg bagels and oranges,
I walk the field out back, through goldenrod,
clover, and purple loosestrife to cross a bridge.

I lose the past with each plant counted,
look for what is new and sticks out.
A dead possum floats belly up in a hole.

A plane stitches the sky
in and out of clouds; the swooping
birds drop a feather on my foot.

I collect seven see-through cicada wings,
dry leaves crusted by the side of my path.
A bold butterfly floats on cottonwood fuzz.

Grass blows east and then west
and I wonder which fresh thing to hold,
how to stay alert in all this turning.

DEER SHIFT

When the deer arrives, I am going slow.
I am tooling down Gunn Road in my
slick new car. It is no design of mine,
an accident, I tell you, that we hit

head on, deer darting smack into
hard metal. It is a leap of faith
and we spin together, deer eyes on
my eyes for a split moment in time.

We join worlds, animal and white car,
me in a spin with freeze-frame of eyes,
a blur of nature and artifice climbing
the windshield in layers of fear,

and all the animals in me climb
out of steel blue velour seats,
out of turbo and fuel injected sighs,
bumper to bumper with the same sky.

For now, deer and I merge in a
theater of meadow. I gather my
skirts and lunge for the trees.
My angular knees bob like broken

sticks, while there, on the exit
ramp of I75, a deer is late for class,
comes cruising in, shaken, to give
an advanced placement test for English 131.

SONIC BLOOM

*In spring and autumn swallows produce vibrations as they flock in a body
of air, causing currents with their wing beats. These and bird song have a
powerful effect on the flowering and fruiting of plants.*

Rudolph Steiner

They're fooling the plants in Florida,
making orange trees blossom
like the opening up of umbrellas.
Planned sounds of flapping

bird wings are broadcast coyly
out of little black boxes in orchards.
Simulated bird songs trill
automatically in pre-dawn concerts

mocking the special sounds,
mocking the combinations of
harmonies and frequencies
flowing from sun up into morning.

Pretending to be birds
these black boxes soar
without moving, swoop and sing
stone still on sticks.

The orange trees shudder
wanting to be one with all
that circles and weaves around them.
The oranges gasp and obey.

RIDING THE ROUND POOL

Producing fire, producing cold, the fountain is reached.
T'ai Hsuan Ching

A purling fountain gurgles and drips
thin strips of clear water
from the mouths of little bat fish.

Moving rainbows spread in fiery
concentric circles around the pool,
under the shadows of floating leaves.

Thoughts drift downstream where memories
hold still. A cicada wobbles nearby,
flies in fast to perch his weight

on a wet branch, plows the dream
with tiny legs aflutter, then stops,
riding the green stem home.

GRACE

trees line up in
stiff rows, bare
in winter, their arms
reach out like
quiet angels, their
gesture delicate, thin
a wire whisper
a winged heart
hope translucent as dust
but silver in
its touching
wish for spring

A NATURAL SLICE

In front of my bay window, people
are seen dragging dead trees.
I watch and it is not easy
to forgive them their confusion.

The moving day sits
still on its trees, and I
am writing as fast as I can
to catch up with the red cardinal
eating yesterday's seeds in suet.

Sometimes a cardinal pecks
at the glass window, a sure sign
that anything fresh might happen
and winter isn't at all sure which
way to turn or what, if any,
current rearrangement works.

And once I get the particulars
down, with my easy lift-off
correcting cassette, I can change
the whole thing anyway. So why
should any dead trees matter?
Why do the dead trees still hurt?

YOU CAN GET TO TOTAL FROM HERE

Like a snake shedding your skin, you rise
up the ragged rungs. A wax
rope ladder leads you higher.

Each step becomes a wish, a pale picture
in a book of knowledge you reach for.
Once a tree stood in your way.

How do I fly through a tree?
you wonder. *How do I crack*
a wooden question with my teeth?

Branch upon branch...this is
no simple dance by numbers.
One foot glued to the floor, you climb.

SPRING LURCH

The lights grow brighter as the earth lurches away from the sun.
F. Scott Fitzgerald

The day among circles. The no-end day
that has flowers in its teeth.
We all gather in the gazebo and
the earth turns once more.

Finding new ground is the caterpillar's
way of dealing with time. Slowly
it is a new root and we are wrung out.

Each blade of grass waits its turn
and grows in a pattern of silence.
The buds. The blossoms. A falling
gypsy moth hangs by its thumbs.

SUN BLOCK

Our real skin knows
we can't erase the sun.
No dab from a tube,
no lube job lets us hide
inside from ultra violet
blast. The past illusions

cook and bubble up.
We hide in dank caves,
court the darling
sleep of fettered fools.
Our comfort smarts in
anesthetic pillows of dark.

We screen ourselves in,
lollygag about the sun porch
with our number ten protection,
lie on beaches lathered
to the hilt with guilt,
while through the labyrinth

creeps the epidermal risk,
the unrestricted exposure
of the fair uncovered parts,
the secret skin flicks,
the final lap where we
go for the burn.

BREAKING THE SILENCE

We are the bees of the invisible.
Rilke

Things heat up. Trees
stick to the sky. Birds
fly through dead brush
to the ceaseless echo drone
of bees in a slight wind.

Don't move. Wait for a
clear note. But the mind
is stuck shut, and still a
melody of birds, melody of sweat
floats through invisible windows.

The pressure mounts, a tight
heart pulling. The stuffy air
inside wants to explode. Swarms
of white bees fly, weave cross
patterns, spinning a web.

A lock breaks. The close fitting
heart alone explodes like
shattered possible glass; a spray
of cut diamonds, fractals, magnifies
the hot bursts of light.

FIRE ON THE LAKE

Green Lady tells the fire department
she sees it out her family room window.
The lake, she tells them, *is burning*
and the flames are one hundred feet high.

Miller Roberts doesn't believe it.
Don't call me, he says, *without proof.*
I can't send men out with their
rubber boots on for nothin', you know.

But the trees, Green Lady warns him,
are bending and getting scorched in smoke.
I see the red flames rising now
as I speak. I see it from my own kitchen.

She doesn't impress him, but he stops
the poker game, and sends out Horace
and Will to appease her. Green Lady
lives on Hunter's Ridge in Wilderness Valley.

The men humor her, as they all
plod through the banks of Lake Elizabeth.
Don't see nothin' here, they choke.
Bet you were lookin' out the wrong window.

But I saw what I saw, she says.
Sometimes these fires burn themselves out.
We like to know where they are, says Will,
so we can stifle them quickly.

Green Lady tells how last night she came
down to the flames with her flashlight.
How she crossed the little bridge at Minnetonka,
so no one would think she was dreaming.

How, even though there are no signs,
no flames, and no smell where flames have been,

she knows what she knows, and proof will rise up.
The lake *is* burning in the moonlight.

Next day she's in the True Value Hardware
buying screws for her storm windows.
Hey, we put a plane over, says Will,
and found fire in the pine forest.

You gotta watch out for those illusions,
says Green Lady. *Something real might grab you.*

BEAT THE DEADLINE — OR LOSE OUT!

It's official. My deceased father
has won the grand sweepstakes again.
How he enters them is a mysterious
feat from the other side.

Open at once! the envelope shouts,
reminding him that his response
is required post haste, a warning
only the deeply buried can appreciate.

If he does not claim his cash
or the new Pontiac Grand Am
(that is already his) he will
automatically lose everything.

Even the dead, it seems, can't escape
eligibility for very big prizes.
They can be instructed, like the living,
to obey the official rules (enclosed).

This is not a joke, or too good
to be true, and my missing father's
chances of winning are far
better than average. Let me explain.

No questions will be asked.
These are the *Everybody Wins
Sweepstakes*, and death is no
excuse for failing to act promptly.

PRAYER FOR THE DEAD AND THE LIVING

But the serious part of prayer begins when we have got our
begging over with and listen...

W.H. *Auden*

One instant it happens, on a
plain Friday in January,
that you are done wanting.

Morning sun flickers on snow
piled high on a summer picnic table
and your old dog isn't hungry.

The wind chill factor is twenty below
and you can't get cold anymore.
Praise everything...is the new order.

The worn rug. The blender. The sink.
Bless one shadow at a time
and circle the moment.

SILENT EXPECTATION

There is a gentle rising up
in the fertile energy of the human
heart, a movement so subtle and moist
it may take weeks to transform
itself to green stem and bud,
but hour by silent hour it stirs
within the darkened loam
an electric possibility,
a great and precious hope
that breaks through crusted
barren soil, with the very momentum
of expectation, into red tulip.

III.
HEART SPILLS

*Inside violins, the music
hides, and sequined paper
notes pile up like dried roses.
History of fire. History of miracles.*

*The heart spills its lonely treasures
and words spin into trophies.
A milagro on a Spanish necklace,
a metal heart, opens like luck.*

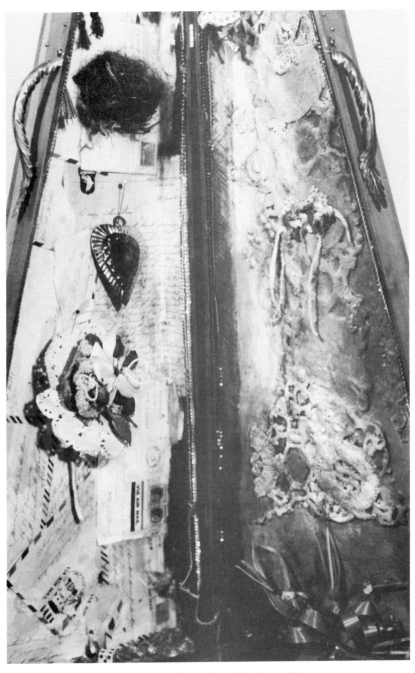

"Amor," (detail) mixed media
Christine Reising, 1991

(hidden agenda)

thank you for this flowered night
fall that spills me into dreams,
thank you for dreams themselves,
who mount horses and rear up
larger than white Clydesdales,
thank you for more skin than I need
to cushion my rubber body when falling,
for falling itself, and the crush of
love bargains I make with the earth,
for the story the earth makes, the dirty
jokes the blue hills make, and mountains,
thank you for every sky I can point to,
thank you for fingernails and cutting
corners, thank you for long hair and
getting lost, for glasses of milk and silk
underwear, for unexpected lovers and
fire, and the lasting, intangible rain

LETTER TO A SOLDIER

I don't know you, but
you're my brother or my son.
My lover who can't see me.
I send you this CARE package
of bent words to open,

words laced with life and sentences
wrapped tight in little griefs,
baked illusions with foil, wrinkled
paragraphs of hope and home
biscuits for you to chew.

We are all tied together with strings.
Across the infinite gulf of time,
the parched deserts of anger
and stubborn refusal to budge,
I send you this small breath
of vowels and constraints,

a letter as a way to win
wars inside the mind, to open
a porthole. A heart
has eyes like beacons
to see between the lines.

We pardon each other, gruffly,
on reams of thin paper.

THE DAY EVERYTHING GOT LOUDER

I pick up a stone that looks like an ear. The ear says, *Don't talk. I'm hard and closed. If you talk, I can't hear you. And if you listen to my words, you're a fool.* Ear talks so much I think I'm hearing a train, a train going fast through a dark tunnel of shadows, a train being sucked through a tube like the money tube at the drive-in bank. *You don't hear a train,* says Ear. But I do. I do. It gets louder and turns green. The train is growing branches like a tree. Leaves and blossoms, roots and a tangled trunk. Tree grows faster than my own ear can listen. It has thick moss and hanging vines, with even a bird. Yes, a bird sings in this very tree. It's a morning bird that warbles and trills. A waterfall of sound cascades, and that stone ear listens and knows. And we still don't talk about it. And we both hear a wild orchid growing.

ROOM SERVICE

Looking into things, I see a late October afternoon.
My shoe in the sunlight, in the Toledo Hilton Hotel,
makes a shadow not unlike the shape of Nebraska.
My coat is sitting sideways in the China-blue chair

leaning right, as if I have just flown out of it
and, perched on the ceiling, proceeded to watch myself.
Doing this allows me an aerial view of my own reasons,
and I say, *What are you doing down there?*

You have your life and you're still afraid.
What lurks in spoons and on the tops of cups
from this morning's "Eye Opener" still throws you.
Sit quietly, I say. And you will be served

sliced pineapple and honeydew in a long-stemmed glass.
The crumpets are coming. The seasonal fruit.
At this point you will sign for it.
You will sign for any fresh thing that arrives.

You've checked the box for appropriate delivery time.
You've circled and circled the items desired.
A little wait, I say from the top of the lamp shade.
A little silence before the knock on your door.

ON THE AIR

Look into the monitor, he says,
You're on the air. Beep Beep.
Start. I look smack into my own
face. She wants to know me, so I
look away, down at the page,
then up, and oh, there
she is again, nosy and persistent.

She's heard this one before, I think.
Why does she look so intense?
How could anyone fall for that
fecund face she puts on?
She must be trying to undress me.
I stare her down with my power glare.

Her voice begins to lift and
swallow my typewriter. Something about
bats in her hair and a diaphanous
tribe of forty year old women
hiking up their panty hose.

I start to get interested.
Maybe she's got something
I could use in my next act.
The air between us is electric.
I forget about the humongous wart
on the side of her nose and her
overbite, the nervous edge to her lip.

Maybe I can love her mistakes.
Wait'll she hears this one,
I think. A ventriloquist
takes over the whole thing and
throws a green poem out of my mouth;
aims it right into her flinching eye.

PILLOW PROMENADE

Sleep faster; we need the pillows.
Yiddish Proverb

Little gray mice are creeping
around inside my head,
watching videos on my eyelids,
taking care not to wake me
by guffawing at my life.

In comes a nude fan dancer
whose feathers catch fire on stage.
I call out, as my car sinks
deep into muddy quicksand,
Wait in ribbons for the ice man!

Lace curtains, bric-a-brac,
finally a kitchen light goes on.
Some tittering is heard in the balcony
as a mouse enters, looking for food.
He finds only stale fig bars and seltzer.

Banquets fly through thin air unnoticed.
The mice whimper to no one special
about our hero's hunger. The bare facts.
Strangely, I go on sleeping faster,
toss and mumble when the re-runs begin.

IT'S RAINING MANIAC WOMEN

"'It's raining maniac women!' said Dave Simons of Stormville,
New York, as 79 sky diving women joined in a record
breaking chain in the air, only a few hours after 73 of them
had snapped the previous mark."
                                    Chicago Tribune, August 1989

Out of moving planes, we
leap in circles, carrying
our children's lunch boxes and
The Hite Report on Women in Love.

From a list of "Fall Essentials"
we order the basic top,
the basic bottom, and
our sky blue aerobic socks.

Budgets that balance make us
wary of ourselves, so we
wear Deep Woods Off, and go
into the Forest Mall daily.

We buy novelty suits from
famous makers, casual
twill and lamb leather pants,
run Stop signs in our
private label sling-backs.

Seeking out a glimmer of hope,
we order clomipramine,
a new drug for holistic women
with the overwhelming urge
to pull out their hair.

THE RED BILLBOARD

She said it was a monument.
She said she felt red in her heart.
She wanted to get to know red,
to see it change in all the seasons.
That was why she had the billboard built
in the apple orchard out back.
That was why the neighbors thought
they might have to have her put away.
The neighbors thought a billboard ought
at least to have a saying on it.
They wondered what it meant,
this fiery rectangle shouting
at the pigeons and the swallows.
And what was it doing so far away
from the highway, or even the dirt road?
She used to spray it down with a hose.
Red when it rained, red dry, and even
redder in the sun. Red was a sign,
she said. And no one dared to ask
what it was a sign of, or why she howled
out there in the orchard in the moonlight.
Red in the winter, red red on the cusp of spring.
Her billboard shouted *RED!* to all the jet planes.
It said, *I'm alive*, to bare clouds and the wind.
It said, *Here I am sky. I'm the color of Yes.*

THE NEW CREAM

The time my mother taught me
about the new cream, she said,
Try this. It's better than anything.
Your skin will know what I mean.

By now, I've tried them all.
I've flaked and scratched my rough
edges under every notion on the shelf.
Everything soaks in, but doesn't change things.

Wait, she said. *You won't believe it,*
but my arms are changing.
They don't hurt anymore, and I can
hold them up into the west wind.

I watch her arms as she tells it.
I watch her know light years with her arms.
I watch the sun come up on the torn quilt
as she tells directions to Demings, the one store

that carries the miraculous new cream,
and I now know what I love in this unique day.
I love the particular itself, and how
to own it is to know something so well

that you can hold everything,
one at a time, in your own rough arms.
Slowly. Without pain.
And in tune with your wild mother.

SURFACING

A woman in the kitchen
begins turning into a canoe.
The tide comes in, and she,
buoyant from holding her own

in the turbulence of wild waves,
begins to float miraculously
up, above the toaster and micro-
wave oven. Small 3x5 cards with
recipes for braised lamb shanks

with oregano and feta, or home
smoked chicken salad, swim
around her, doing the lean breast
stroke, begging her to surrender.

Like a tropical sweet potato
she's waited years for this.
Brushing the crushed pineapple
from her hair, she grows oars

and, as if guided by an
inspired flounder, makes her way
effortlessly through the lace
of kitchen gadgets promising life.

She's spent years soaked
up in her life, like a ziti
with marinara sauce, and now,
now with this simple gesture,

this frivolous escape from
the frequent shoppers' day old
baked goods bargain table,
she floats, unbreaded and free

above it all, higher
than a nacho grande,
more delicate than mahi mahi
with lime and papaya salsa,

surfacing with her own dilled life,
a battered canoe that won't tip.
Her curved resiliency built in,
she's creating herself from scratch.

I VACUUM, THEREFORE I AM

Life sucks order from a sea of disorder.
James Gleick, *Chaos*

If I could glean a drop
of wild intent from the inevitable flurry
of chaos blowing in my life,
if I could pull into the vacuum
enough clear order to fill a bag
with paper party hats and dust,

I could make a song to this dust.
I could sing it while dropping
my kids off at the Burger King, I could bag
the first angry housewife, tell her in a flurry
of glorious abstractions to uphold the vacuum,
that we now have the answer to our lives,

tell her that to understand her life
she needs to number and color code the dust,
needs to realize that with her vacuum
comes the essence of what drops
through the cosmos in a wild flurry.
It comes into her very own Eureka bag.

I could tell her not to throw away that bag.
One look at the serious pattern of life
inside the scum she sucks up in a flurry,
even the tiniest particle of dust,
could solve biology's basic mystery, drop by drop.
Non-linear dynamics loves a vacuum.

I'd tell her she is the queen of her upright vacuum,
pattern born from formlessness, an old bag
discovering her youth, with memories dropping
like torn movies through the fuzzy boundaries of her life.
Tell her the stream of order in that inscrutable dust
will come to her, in a dark dream, in a flurry

while cleaning the breakfast plates, in a flurry
of ideas running in the hose of her vacuum.
O living, continuous housewife, understand dust,
recycle it, carefully filling each bag,
challenging the twist on the mystery of life,
and savor each existential drop.

Order comes from disorder. Dust in a paper bag.
The flurry dances in your vacuum.
We suck life till we drop.

FOOD FROM THE HEART

My brother, who can't write
his own letters, sends me cheese
for Christmas. "Cheese from Jon"
says the card inside the package
I find inside the side door.

Jon is at it again, I think.
In Watertown, Wisconsin, living
in a home for the helpless,
the less apt, the retarded,
he sends me greetings and cheese.

In another life he was to be
my little smart-assed brother.
He was meant to tattle on me,
or punch my lights out if I told
who pulled the front legs off frogs.

Instead, at forty five, he drives
an electric wheel chair through
the streets of his silence, nods
and points to get his way,
has a nurse to wipe his drool.

This year the letters started.
*Hey, Sis. I'm having
a great day. It's a little
cool outside. I love the toy
gun you sent. Well, I gotta go.*

I've tried to write him back,
even sent a tape of family trivia.
But it all feels like cheese,
Colby or Baby Swiss with holes.
Somehow I know he gets the joke.

Sitting all these years inside
his own maze, he's learned
to laugh at the drop of a
Christmas Muenster. The look in his
eye says it all. *Don't pity*

me. I know my Monterey Jack.
I'll send you a sharp
Cheddar for the new year.
I'm OK in here. Read my lips.
Spread this on crackers.

USED CLOTHES

At night, our dead visit us in used clothes.
They wander the halls wearing the dusky
fabric of words that echo like bats
sensing the boundaries of their way in.

My father comes wearing a Chinese silk robe
from the hospital thrift shop, dragging a machine
that feeds him glucose through a tube in his neck.
His dark eyes burn like votive candles.

It's not over, he tells me, weakly.
Stepping out of our bodies is a trick we do
with antique mirrors to confuse you.
The dead swim in designer jeans with torn labels.

Sometimes we wear their clothes like cowboy shirts
to a rodeo, hats to keep our corduroy regrets covered.
We curl inside them, use them as a comforter,
a patchwork of velvet intrusions.

Sometimes the dead bring us their laundry,
like children with their plastic baskets of need,
or like masked robbers, they tie us up and leave us
to eat moth balls on chipped centennial plates.

I'm tired of giving this poem to the dead,
tired of walking in their wing-tipped shoes.
I want to deliver this to you in my bare skin,
wearing the blunt nakedness of the living.

EMBRACING THE FALL

The body, tumbling through space,
faces a kind of enigma: sometimes
falling down can clear things up.
Limbs flying, an ungraceful arch,
it tries to brace itself, defy
gravity, prevent the little invasions
of iced sidewalk or parquet floor,
the slap of indignant boundaries.

A faint, a momentary vasovagal
dizziness can bring it on,
as if the spin of the earth
needs to jettison one body in motion,
thrown like jetsam from a ship,
like unwanted goods bailed out
to lighten the overload.

Now the fall becomes its own
remedy for weakness. Getting
lost is a new way to be found.
The splat, the horizontal daze,
no longer preventable,
becomes a lush embrace, a
hardy hug of jeweled stimuli
to flatten any resistance,
bringing the hard head down,

down to the level of the heart,
where blood and dreams can travel
over the parched road map,
the jet stream of resilience,
the unbound butterfly in the brain.

THE WELL MAN

The well man came with his tools,
drove his rig up my front lawn,
began a granular plunge
through frozen earth and clay.
Through gravel, sand, and silt,
he meant to get to the bottom,
to find the tip of frozen pump,
rusted iron parts gone numb.

He knew the water was there.
He said, Be patient. Be calm,
and dug for hours and days,
heard a motor hum and drive
him deeper into the well.
Inside, dry faucets groaned.
A trickle, a gasp, and then
silence. A parched bath.

He knew the water was there.
He said his tools were adequate,
that I should not watch him work,
and as the earth crumbled in,
I should take my showers
at the Royal Spartan Motel.

He knew the water was there.
It was like reading a palm,
he said, through stars and crosses,
through heart line, life line,
a mystic triangle of dirt.
Just like making angels in snow,
wrapping chains around an old hurt
tire, he pulled and rattled his truck,

and then the flood came,
Artesian bubble and flow,

80

Niagara falling at every stop.
Faucets shook at the spring
push, real proof of divining rods,
a release of irrepressible rain.

WRITING FOR THE CHURCH

When I wrote for God,
I had to wear stockings each day.
It was ecumenical, and my Word
Perfect hummed along. I believed
I could touch God with a motion of my fingers.
It was almost like praying.

Words were a diaphanous prayer,
I thought, and formed my impression of God's
wisdom. I guessed at it with my fingers
flying over the keyboard each day.
I hardly knew what I believed,
but then, as word piled upon word,

I soon ran out of perfect words.
I began to feel another prayer
growing in the dark center of my belief.
It said, *Where are you, God?*
to the air around my IBM. One day
I canceled the words. I fingered

the silences, the spaces where no fingers
could call up the texture of words.
That, I suddenly knew, was the day
I surrendered the structure of prayer.
I gave up trying to figure out God.
It was a new slant on believing.

I could let go of my belief
that anyone had a holy finger
on the truth, or could out-guess God.
I even let go of the word
absolute. The word *open* became a prayer
simpler to stitch into my see-through daze.

Now this is a startling new day-
time habit of mine, this gauzy belief
that any two random thoughts are prayers
that might cross my mind like two fingers
crossed for luck. I think any words
that stick together might approximate God.

Now I look for loose prayers. I fold my fingers
each day around the keys. I believe
I'm searching for the unbounded, a wordless God.

CHEAP THRILLS

for Brian Swimme

Turning a somersault on a cloudy day. There is no shadow, not a trace to be found of anything lost.

Chinese Proverb

Looking for a new front entrance
I went to Peacock Alley door store.
It was a maze of oak and pine
thresholds. Walking through felt
like stepping into time.

Beveled glass and leaded Victorian
windows drew me like a cumulus cloud
through and through each new
portal, each gate an omen
portending the next point of entry.

Trying to be outgoing and cuddlesome,
I began turning somersaults in order to
randomly access any forms of radiant
energy that might drift by.
Sunshine came and went, leaving
only canary yellow traces, no
shadows to get lost in.

It took eight weeks to install my
chosen door, the one with glass
ripples to divide the sun
in portions on my vestibule wall.
Mornings I puzzle at the posh
circle of light, see how lucky I am
to stand bedazzled in the hall.

AS IF WONDROUS

I make my way through foggy streets, as if
wondrous, as if I were made of brittle
glass particles that float just over a cement
sidewalk, as if all my loose parts might
glisten and the sound gatherings of wind
might willow through me, as if Tuesday
and the other instant facts of my life
could arrange themselves, quietly
in sequential order, calm as a
cat; as if purring, I could decide to allow
telephone poles their freedom to be stuck,
allow grass, that keeps growing, into my life
at random intervals, as if I could have the power
to open my own two eyes, as if wonder
were a loaf of bread that would keep
rising, as if hope were a red cardinal
that would never smash into my porch.

ABOUT THE AUTHOR

Margo LaGattuta lives in Rochester, Michigan. Her earlier books include: **Diversion Road**, 1983, State Street Press; Noedgelines, 1986, Earhart Press; and **The Dream Givers**, 1990, Lake Shore Publishing. Her poems have won numerous awards and appeared in many literary journals and anthologies. She has received teaching grants from the Michigan Council for Art and Cultural Affairs, Comerica Bank and the Friends of the Detroit Public Library and was nominated for the 1993 Michigan Author Award. Her essays have appeared in assorted newspapers and magazines. The "Noedgelines" exhibit, a collaboration with visual artist Christine Reising, has traveled to thirteen galleries in Michigan, Illinois and Canada.

Margo has an MFA in Poetry from Vermont College; teaches writing workshops at Oakland Community College, Cranbrook, and many galleries and universities; and is a writing consultant for schools and teachers. Her business, Inventing the Invisible (29 West Lawrence, Pontiac, Michigan 48342) produces seminars, audio tapes, videos, note cards, calendars, t-shirts and mugs. Her weekly radio program, "Art in the Air," is broadcast on WPON, 1460 AM, from Bloomfield Hills, Michigan.

ABOUT THE ARTIST

Visual artist, Christine Reising, resides in Ann Arbor, Michigan and has been teaching drawing and painting at Siena Heights College in Adrian for the last ten years. In addition to teaching, she has been Director of their Klemm Gallery producing more than fifteen exhibitions yearly. Reising has exhibited extensively throughout the Midwest and Canada including at the Artemesia Gallery (Chicago, Ill), the Women's History Museum and the Kresge Art Museum (Lancing, MI), the Art Gallery of Windsor (Ontario, Canada) and the Evansville Museum of Art (Evansville, Indiana).